SOME PIGTAILS

A *Lola Jones* BOOK

JONATHAN EIG

illustrated by
ALICIA TEBA GODOY

ALBERT WHITMAN & CO.
Chicago, Illinois

For Lillian, Jeffery, and Lola—JE

To every girl that stands for something—ATG

Library of Congress Cataloging-in-Publication data
is on file with the publisher.

Text copyright © 2020 by Jonathan Eig
Illustrations copyright © 2020 by Albert Whitman & Company
Illustrations by Alicia Teba Godoy
Hardcover edition first published in the United States of America
in 2020 by Albert Whitman & Company
Paperback edition first published in the United States of America
in 2020 by Albert Whitman & Company
ISBN 978-0-8075-6564-3 (hardcover)
ISBN 978-0-8075-6568-1 (paperback)
ISBN 978-0-8075-6566-7 (ebook)

Printed in the United States of America
10 9 8 7 6 5 4 3 2 1 LB 24 23 22 21 20

Design by Aphelandra Messer

For more information about Albert Whitman & Company,
visit our website at www.albertwhitman.com.

TABLE OF CONTENTS

1.
Getting Ready
for School

"Where are you going with that brush?" Lola's mother asked her one Monday morning before school.

"Downstairs to see Grampa," said Lola, who was eight and a half. She had a pink plastic hair brush and a bag of elastic bands in one hand and her favorite book, *Charlotte's Web*, in the other.

"Why are you bringing a brush?" her mother asked.

"Well," Lola said, "you're too busy to do pigtails today and I can't do them myself, so I'm going to ask Grampa."

1

Lola's mother put a peanut-butter-and-banana sandwich in a brown bag. "Grampa doesn't get up this early, Lola. You know that. Also, I don't think he knows how to make pigtails."

"He might," Lola said, and she sang a song as she skipped out the door of her apartment and down a flight of stairs to the first floor of her building. That's where her grandfather lived.

Lola opened the door with a key she wore on a string around her neck and went in. Grampa Ed had an art studio in the front of his apartment and a bedroom and kitchen at the back. Grampa's apartment smelled of smoke and ink and glue and paint and coffee and Grampa.

Lola was dressed neatly in her school uniform— a white shirt with a blue skirt—but her brown hair was a tangled mess. She went into Grampa's bedroom. "Knock-knock," Lola said, because she knew her grandfather liked knock-knock jokes.

"Nobody's home," Grampa Ed said from under a pile of blankets in bed.

"No, Grampa, you're supposed to say 'who's there?'!" Lola said.

"'Who's there?' is only for people who arrive at a civilized hour," came Grampa's voice from beneath the covers. "Come back at noon and we'll find out who's there."

"But I *need* you, Grampa!" Lola said. "I *really, really* need you!"

"Get lost, kid."

"But I have a surprise for you," Lola said. "Get up, Grampa!"

"A surprise? You've got nothing I want. No money, no beer, no White Sox tickets..."

"I'll read *Charlotte's Web* to you!" Lola said, holding up her book.

"No thanks," Grampa said. "Any other ideas?"

"Not yet, but I'm sure I'll think of something," Lola said. She stood there by Grampa Ed's bed, rubbing her chin as she thought.

Then Lola tossed her book on the bed and jumped on top of her grandfather's mountain of a back. She threw her arms around him and said, "*C'mon*, wake up, Grampa!"

"Hey, you're heavy," he said.

Lola jumped off the mountain, her sneakers landing on a red plastic cup that made a cracking noise.

"Now get up!" she said. "My whole day depends on an important job I have for you."

Grampa Ed stuck his head out from under the covers and raised a fuzzy eyebrow. He looked at his granddaughter's smile, with its missing tooth on top and dimpled cheeks, and almost smiled too. "This better be good," he said as he moaned and pushed up from his bed.

Lola held out her pink hairbrush and the plastic bag full of colored elastic bands.

4

"Can you make pigtails?" she asked.

Grampa Ed sighed. He wore a white sleeveless T-shirt and Mickey Mouse pajama bottoms. His head was bald on top, but he had white hair on the sides of his head and a thick white mustache and beard. His arms were covered with tattoos, including a big one on his left bicep that read, *Whatever Lola Wants*.

"Do I look like a guy who makes pigtails?" Grampa Ed scratched both armpits at the same time and then sniffed his fingertips. "What's a pigtail, anyway?" he asked.

"Grampa! You know!"

"Why would I ask if I knew? Anyway, make me some coffee or get on your way to school."

Lola loved making coffee. She put a scoop of beans in a grinder and poured water into Grampa Ed's electric kettle.

"Your feet smell, Grampa," she said.

"I thought my nose smelled," he answered with a shrug.

Lola laughed.

"You're good at jokes, Grampa," she said. "And you could be good at pigtails, too. You could be really good. Didn't you tell me you learned to tie fancy knots when you were in the gravy?"

"Navy."

"Whatever. Can you make a fancy knot or not?"

"Yeah."

"Plus, you're an artist. And that means you

like colors. And look how many colors of elastic bands I have!"

Lola pointed to the bag of elastic bands on Grampa Ed's night table. She went back to making coffee. Lola put coffee grinds in a paper cone, put the cone over a cup, and poured water into the cone. She turned water to coffee like magic!

"Here," she said, handing her grandfather the hairbrush and the big bag of brightly colored elastic bands. "While the coffee's dripping, part my hair, and put each side in an elastic band. Twist the band around the hair until it's tight. It's simple."

"Why didn't you say so? I could have finished this conversation a long time ago and gone back to sleep."

"But then we wouldn't have had all this fun!" Lola said.

Grampa Ed took a big breath, in and out, but he didn't speak. He took the brush in one hand and a handful of elastic bands in the other. While

he worked, Lola silently read *Charlotte's Web*. Maybe she could have a pet pig someday. And a pet spider too.

Several minutes later, Grampa Ed was done. "There," he said. "Best I can do."

Lola closed her book, picked up the coffee cup, handed it to her grandpa, kissed his cheek, and skipped out of the room.

"Don't you want to look at my work?" Grampa Ed called after her. "There's a mirror in the bathroom."

"No thanks," Lola said. "I trust you. Anyway, it's late. I have to go. See you after school, Grampa. Love you!"

Grampa Ed lifted his coffee cup to his lips and took a slurpy sip. Lola went back upstairs to her apartment. As she walked in, her mother came from the kitchen holding a waffle and a backpack.

"Let's go, sweetie," she said.

"Do you like my pigtails, Mom?" Lola asked.

"Uh-huh, they're adorable," her mother said without looking. Lola knew her mother was a little nervous because it was her first day on a new job. Lola's mother used to be a police officer, but now she was one of the people who told other police officers what to do. She was a supervisor. Even though the title had the word "super" in it, Lola thought the new job sounded boring. Driving around in a police car was much more fun than sitting at a desk and going to meetings.

Lola and her mother held hands as they walked. When they got to school, Lola kissed her mother goodbye. Mom made a funny face when she finally looked at Lola's hair but didn't say anything. Lola's friends Maya and Fayth ran to greet her.

"Whoa!" said Maya.

"Whoa! Whoa!" said Fayth.

Both girls giggled.

"What?" asked Lola.

"What happened to your hair?" Maya and Fayth asked at the same time.

Lola put one hand on each of her pigtails. "I need a mirror," she said.

Lola ran into the school building as fast as she could and slipped into the nearest girls' room. She rushed to the sinks, looked up, and froze. There, staring back at her in the mirror, was Lola, eyes wide open, mouth making an "O," with two pigtails sticking out as straight and stiff as the handlebars on a bicycle. Both were wrapped so heavily in red, white, and blue rubber bands that only the tips of Lola's brown hair poked out from the ends.

A smile crept across Lola's face.

"Whoa! Whoa! Whoa!" she said as Maya and Fayth stood there grinning. "Cool!"

2.
Dinner

At dinner that night, Lola still had her red-white-and-blue pigtails.

"These things are unbelievable!" she told her mother and grandfather as they ate spaghetti with garlic bread. "They never even came loose! I did monkey bars. I wrestled in the dirt with that mean boy James. I got my whole face wet in the third-floor water fountain that sprays a mile high! But these pigtails never got messed up!"

"When I make a knot, it stays a knot," Grampa said. "That's what they teach you in the gravy."

"Thanks, Grampa. I got *sooo* much attention today!"

"And that's a good thing?" he asked.

"Of course!"

Lola looked at her mother. "Mom," she said, "may I be excused for a second?"

"But you haven't finished your dinner," her mother said.

"I'll be right back, I promise!"

Lola's mother nodded, and Lola jumped up from the table. She ran to her room and came back with a sheet of paper. She read it out loud. "From now on, every Monday I want these American flag handlebar pigtails. On Tuesdays I want a high ponytail. On Wednesdays I want a side pony. On Thursdays I want front pigtails. And on Friday you can do whatever you want."

Grampa Ed had his face two inches from his plate, slurping up a strand of spaghetti that had escaped his fork.

"Who can do whatever who wants?" he asked, looking up.

"You!" Lola said. "Friday's your day to be creative."

"What are you talking about?"

"This is a list of the ponytails and pigtails I want every day," she said. "But on Friday you get to do whatever you want."

Grampa Ed wiped his mouth. He turned to look at Lola's mother first, and then at Lola.

"No," he said. "Uh-uh."

"Please?" Lola asked.

"No."

"Why not?"

"Lola," Mom said, "Grampa said he doesn't want to."

"But why?" Lola asked.

"First of all," Grampa said, "I don't take orders from little people, even if they're cute little people who make good coffee. Second of all, I've got better things to do."

"Like what?" Lola asked.

"Lola," Mom said, "that's disrespectful."

"Sorry, Mom. Sorry, Grampa."

Everyone chewed in silence for a few minutes. But Lola was thinking as she chewed. She was thinking of *Charlotte's Web*—of the little girl in the story, Fern. Fern was eight years old, just like Lola. In the story, Fern was determined to do what she felt was right, and she came up with a way to convince her father to see her point of view. If her father allowed her to have her way, then Fern would take on the extra responsibility that came with it. Maybe Lola could convince her grandfather to see her point of view. Maybe she could offer a trade.

"Grampa?" she said.

"Yeah?"

"Grampa, you're really, really good at pigtails. You could be, like, famous or something."

Grampa made a scraping noise in his throat that wasn't pleasant.

"Here's a deal: If you make me pigtails every day, I'll make you coffee every day."

Grampa Ed shook his head.

"Wait!" Lola said. "I'm not done with the deal! How about this? I'll make you coffee every day before you wake up. And I'll make you more when I get home from school."

Grampa Ed smiled. "I want scrambled eggs every Monday, oatmeal on Tuesday, pancakes on Wednesday, biscuits and gravy on Thursday…"

"OK, Grampa," Lola said, "I get it." She thought for a few seconds and then she said, "How about this? You can make me any kind of pigtails you want." She crumpled up her list. "And only on school days."

"Lemme think about it," he said. He took a piece of garlic bread bigger than Lola's hand, used it to swab up the last of his spaghetti sauce, and shoved the whole thing in his mouth. "I don't know if I'm ready for this kind of responsibility," he said with his mouth full.

"You don't have to do it forever," she said.

"That's a relief."

"Just until summer."

Mom said, "How about you both try it tomorrow and see what happens?"

Lola thought about it. Grampa thought about it too.

"Is it a deal?" Lola asked.

Grampa made a grunting sound.

"OK," Lola said. "We'll try it tomorrow." And then she whispered so no one could hear: "Tomorrow infinity."

The next morning, Lola got dressed while her mother was in the shower, tiptoed down to Grampa Ed's apartment, and made coffee. She looked at the clock on the wall, and when it was almost time to leave for school she woke him with a hug.

"I'm ready for my pigtails, Grampa," she sang happily.

3.
A Flashing Light

Lola loved her pigtails. She loved joking with her grandpa in the mornings as he brushed her hair and complained and twisted it into all kinds of shapes.

Every weekday, as soon as she got dressed, she made Grampa Ed's coffee and woke him with a hug and kiss. Every afternoon, she made him another cup of coffee and told him all about what her friends had said about her hair.

ele

Lola's school had a dress code: white shirts and navy pants or skirts. Everyone looked plain and looked the same, which was OK with Lola. She didn't care much about clothes. But for the first few days of Grampa's pigtails, she felt a little special. Maya and Fayth couldn't wait to see what Lola would look like each morning.

Because it was fun and because Lola liked routines, she never looked in the mirror at her pigtails until she got to school. She liked to let Maya and Fayth see first. Together, the girls would run to the bathroom, giggling all the way. After Lola looked in the mirror, the three girls would decide on the best name for that day's hairstyle. The first day was American Flag Handlebars.

The second day was Pink and Purple Waterfalls. The third day they called it the Three Little Pigtails. On the fourth day, Grampa Ed stuck green gum wrappers beneath the hair ties to make tiny bows that smelled like spearmint. They called that one Minty Green. On the fifth day, he wrapped Lola's pigtails around pipe cleaners to make heart shapes. The girls called that one the Heart 2 Heart. On the sixth day, Grampa gave Lola pigtails that looked like they were shooting from the top of her head like the crazy third-floor water fountain at school. That one was named The Fountainhead.

One Friday morning, as Lola sat down at the first row of desks in her classroom, the children behind her were unusually loud.

"Quiet down, please, children," said Mrs. Gunderson, Lola's teacher, who had curly silver hair and a big, wide smile.

The room only got louder.

"Children, *please*!" Mrs. Gunderson said. "You're noisier than my grandchildren, and *they're* only in preschool!"

The room got even louder.

Lola turned around and saw that some of her friends were pointing her way.

"Lola!" said Maya. "There's a flashing light on your head!"

Lola turned but couldn't see it.

Mrs. Gunderson walked over, looked at the back of Lola's head, and said: "Oh, my!"

In the back of Lola's head, wrapped firmly between two pigtails, was a round, red light the size of a quarter. It was the kind of blinking light people used when they rode bicycles at night,

and since Mrs. Gunderson was an expert bicycle rider, she knew exactly how to turn off the light without messing up Lola's hair.

"That will do," she said. "Children...please calm down."

At lunch and recess, almost everyone in Lola's class asked for a chance to turn Lola's light on and off. She let them. But after recess she kept the light off the rest of the day. When the final bell rang and it was time to go home, Mrs. Gunderson stopped Lola at the door and handed her an envelope.

"Lola, honey, would you please give this note to your mother tonight?" she said, with a hand on Lola's shoulder. "You're not in trouble. I just wanted to tell your mother that I love your pigtails—everyone does—even though today's flashing light was a bit of a distraction."

"OK, sure, Mrs. Gunderson," Lola said. "But, well, um…."

Lola wasn't sure whether to say that her grandfather made the pigtails, so she didn't.

"OK, bye!" Lola said as she skipped out the door and down the hall.

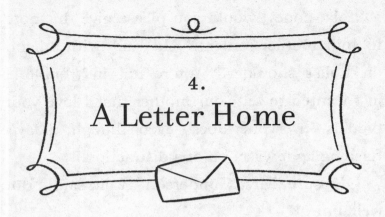

4.
A Letter Home

When Lola got home that afternoon, she dropped Mrs. Gunderson's letter on her grandfather's drawing table.

"What's that?" Grampa Ed asked.

"A letter from my teacher," Lola said.

"You in trouble, kid?"

"No, I think *you* are."

"That so?"

"Maybe."

Grampa was sketching the feet of a bird. He had glued a bunch of things onto his canvas and had drawn a bunch more things. He liked collages. The bird was perched atop a sign that read *Western Avenue New and Used Cars.* The bird was bigger than the sign.

"Why don't you open it and read it to me?" Grampa asked.

Lola opened the envelope and removed a handwritten letter with blue ink on white loose-leaf paper:

Dear Ms. Jones,

When I was a little girl, my father made a robot costume for me on Halloween. The robot costume had a lot of buttons on the front. Some of the buttons lit up and some did nothing. When I was in the library reaching for a book, I noticed a new button. It was on my right shoulder. When I pushed it, a red light blinked and a loud siren began to wail. I couldn't make it stop. Finally, I ripped the button off. When I got home, my father asked me if I had pushed all the buttons on the robot costume. I just smiled at him.

The flashing red light in Lola's hair today reminded me of that robot costume.

I'm enjoying Lola's interesting hairstyles. I'm enjoying her bravery and her creativity.

Fondly,
Sandy Gunderson

Grampa Ed put down his pencil.

"Read that again, would you please?"

Lola did.

Grampa Ed folded the letter and slid it into his desk drawer. He removed a sheet of new paper and started drawing. Lola watched as Grampa drew a robot with spatulas for hands, a police siren on top of its head, and a big, round red button on its shoulder. He handed Lola his pencil.

"Do me a favor, kid," he said. "Under the red button in capital letters, but not too big, write this: "CAUTION. DO NOT PUSH BUTTON IN LIBRARY!"

Then he slid the drawing into an envelope and told Lola to give it to her teacher.

"Tell her it's from your hair stylist," he said.

5.
Saturday

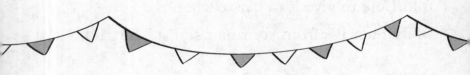

The next day was Saturday.

Lola went to swimming lessons in the morning and a birthday party for her friend Jasmine in the afternoon.

Before the birthday party, Lola's mother took her to a little store on Broadway where they offered 450 different kinds of juice drinks. Lola's mother ordered one with walnuts, raisins, sweet potato, bananas, and milk. Lola got one with orange juice, mango, and strawberries. Lola liked guessing what color her drink would be when all the ingredients got smashed up in the blender, even though they were usually some dull shade of gray or brown.

"Honey," Mom said, "how would you feel about having Grampa walk you to school for a while?"

"Why?"

"My boss wants me to start work earlier in the morning," Mom said.

"I don't mind if Grampa takes me to school," Lola said, "but I'm not sure he's going to like it. And I'm not sure if I can wake him up early. He's grumpy in the morning."

"He's grumpy all day," Mom said. "But if anyone can wake him, it's you. That big guy will do *anything* for you."

Lola smiled. "Was he like that for you when

you were a kid? Would he get up early and do anything for you?"

Now it was Mom's turn to smile. "Yep," she said. "He was a really good daddy. But he didn't make pigtails back then. That's a new talent for him."

"Did he draw pictures for you to give your teachers?"

"No, not that I can remember," Mom said.

When Lola and her mother finished their juices, they took a bus downtown to the bowling alley where Jasmine was having her party. Mom gave Lola a kiss on the top of her head and said she'd be back in three hours. Lola waved goodbye and the girls started bowling.

Soon Jasmine, Maya, Fayth, and Lola were talking and laughing with the other kids at the party and trying to see who could bounce their bowling balls off the bumpers most often on each turn. When Lola's turn came in the seventh frame, Maya screamed:

"Lola! Oh my gosh!"

Lola turned around. "What?" she asked.

"You don't have pigtails today! I just realized!"

"I know," Lola said, and she made a sad face. "It's Saturday, and my Grampa Ed sleeps late on Saturdays and Sundays."

"Well, at least you get pigtails most of the time," Maya said. "I never get them. My hair's too short! I want to grow it longer, but my mom won't let me."

"Why not?" Lola asked.

"She says it's easier to take care of when it's short," Maya said. "My mom has really short hair too."

"Well, that's not fair," Lola said. "You're eight years old. You're old enough to be in charge of your own hair."

"That's not what my mom says," Maya said with a shrug.

"Do you brush your own teeth?" Lola asked.

"Yes," said Maya.

"Do you get dressed by yourself?"

"Yes."

"Do you pick your own nose?"

The girls all laughed.

"Of course!" Maya said.

The girls laughed louder.

Lola folded her arms and raised her voice: "Then you should be able to pick your hair too!"

6.
A Coffee Cup Full of Hair

On Sunday night, after dinner, Lola's mother laid out Lola's school uniform and made her breakfast and lunch. Lola was in bed by eight. She dreamed that night that one of her pigtails held a pencil and the other held an eraser. In the dream, Lola's pigtails did all her homework and got a perfect ten out of ten on her spelling test.

When Monday's morning sun slanted through the blinds, Lola got up and went to her mother's room. Her mother was already dressed and brushing her hair. She wrapped Lola in a hug and kissed her cheek.

"After you get dressed and eat your breakfast, grab your backpack and go down to Grampa's place," Mom said. "He said he would wake up early today to walk you to school."

"OK, Mom," Lola said.

"And just be patient with Grampa today, sweetie," Mom said. "He doesn't like changes in his routine. This isn't going to be easy for him."

Lola promised to be nice. She kissed her mother and skipped downstairs to Grampa Ed's place. Surprise! Grampa Ed was awake. He had already tugged a pair of blue jeans over his pajama pants. Lola was happy to see that Grampa Ed was taking his new job seriously, and she got to work making coffee. Grampa Ed buttoned up a red flannel shirt and put on a gray sweatshirt.

When the coffee was done, Lola delivered the mug and held out a pair of sparkly silver hair ties for her grandfather.

"You're not tired of pigtails yet?" he asked.

"No way!"

"Any requests?" he asked.

"Whatever you want."

"I had kind of a crazy dream last night and it gave me an idea. You mind if I try something? If it's bad, you can take it out."

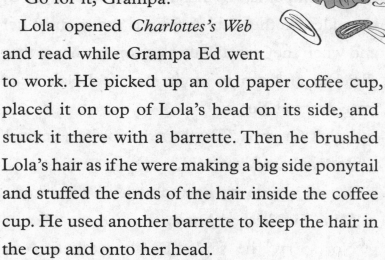

"Go for it, Grampa."

Lola opened *Charlottes's Web* and read while Grampa Ed went to work. He picked up an old paper coffee cup, placed it on top of Lola's head on its side, and stuck it there with a barrette. Then he brushed Lola's hair as if he were making a big side ponytail and stuffed the ends of the hair inside the coffee cup. He used another barrette to keep the hair in the cup and onto her head.

He took a picture on his phone and showed it to her.

"Holy macaroni!" Lola said.

Her hair looked like coffee spilling out of the cup and onto her head.

"You're a genius, Grampa!"

"Not too embarrassing to wear to school?"

"Well, there *is* trash on my head. But it's a work of art! I like it!"

As Lola and Grampa Ed walked out of Grampa's apartment, Lola looked down the block and saw Maya and Fayth coming. Maya was accompanied by her mother, and Fayth by her older brother. Lola's friends ran to meet her, and when they saw the cup on top her head, they shrieked and ran in circles to see Lola's head from every angle.

"Lola's Grampa," Fayth said, "you're a genius!"

"So I've heard," he said.

"Would you do my hair someday?" she asked.

"Mine too?" asked Maya.

"No, sorry," he said. "I only work for one customer."

"Awwwww!" both girls whined.

Maya and Fayth and Lola held hands as they walked. Grampa walked next to Maya's mother but didn't talk to her. He looked a little tired and

not very happy. When they arrived at school, the girls lined up on the playground and waited for Mrs. Gunderson to lead them into the building. When Mrs. Gunderson arrived, she looked at Lola's hair but didn't say anything. Lola handed Mrs. Gunderson the envelope containing her grandfather's drawing.

"This is from my grandfather," she said. "He's over there."

Mrs. Gunderson smiled and gave a big wave to Lola's grandfather. Grampa Ed looked around to see if she was waving to someone else. When he realized there was no one else standing nearby, he offered a small wave in return.

When Lola got home that afternoon, she went straight to Grampa Ed's studio.

"Why do you make pictures for Mrs. Gunderson every time she writes you a letter?" Lola asked.

"Not every time," Grampa Ed said. "Just once."

"But why?"

"Because good letter writing is rare," he said. "And it ought to be rewarded."

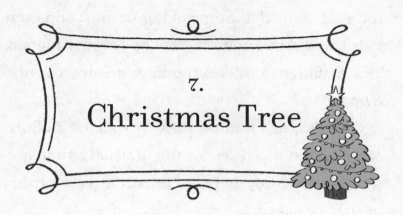

7.
Christmas Tree

As fall slipped into winter, city workers hung snowflakes and wreaths from the lampposts on Broadway, the air grew snappish and cold, and Christmas trees and holiday lights began to appear in the windows of the apartments on Lola's block.

Grampa Ed stopped complaining about making pigtails. Lola had the feeling that he was enjoying it, even though he didn't say so. Grampa Ed received more letters from Mrs. Gunderson, and Mrs. Gunderson received more drawings from Grampa Ed.

At school, Lola became well-known for her

unusual hairstyles. Some of her friends, and even kids she didn't know, began copying her pigtails and making up interesting new designs of their own.

One day, as Grampa Ed was walking Lola to school, he noticed one of the unusual hairstyles.

"Does that boy have a Christmas tree on his head?" he asked.

"I think that's his hair, Grampa," Lola said. "It

looks like he painted it green and used some kind of gel to make it stand up straight."

Lola yelled to the boy: "Hey, Lorenzo! Can I see your hair?"

She ran to meet him.

"That's so cool, Lorenzo! Did you do it yourself?"

"My mom did it," he said. "I asked her to string blinking lights, but that was too much trouble. I told her I got the idea from you."

"My grandpa does my hair," Lola said. "This is my Grampa Ed. Grampa, this is Lorenzo. He's the smartest boy in my class."

"Nice to meet you, sir," Lorenzo said. "Did you really do all of Lola's hairstyles?"

Grampa Ed scratched his bald head and looked at the ground. "Um, I guess so," he said.

"That's awesome," Lorenzo said. "The other day one of your pigtails looked like an Alpine Butterfly Loop. I read about those knots in a book about sailing."

"See, Grampa?" Lola said. "I told you Lorenzo was smart."

"So you did," Grampa said.

The school bell rang.

"Bye, Grampa," Lola said. She stood on her tiptoes, and Grampa Ed bent over for a kiss.

"So long, kid. Have a good day. And, Lorenzo, you take it easy. Don't let any birds land in that Christmas tree."

8.
A Letter from the Principal

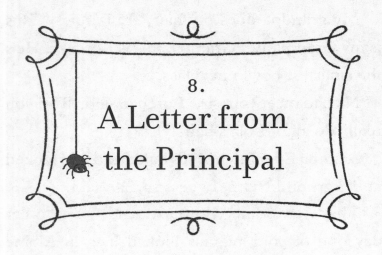

A few days after Christmas, when the children were still on vacation from school, a letter arrived at Lola's house. It was from the principal of her school, Mr. Raymond Murch.

Lillian Jones
1015 Arable St.

Lola's mother read it out loud to Lola and Grampa Ed:

Dear Parents,

As you know, our school has a dress code for students—white collared shirts and blue pants or skirts. The dress code gives us a serious school atmosphere. It helps students concentrate more on their work and less on their clothes. It saves money for families.

We have always encouraged children to express themselves. But in recent weeks, many children have been wearing highly unusual hairstyles. That has caused distractions in some classes. After discussing this with teachers and parents, we have decided to add new language to the dress code so that parents can avoid hairstyles that might get in the way of learning. Beginning in January, when children return to school, they will be allowed to wear only ordinary pigtails and ponytails.

Thank you for your help.

Happy Holidays,
Raymond Murch

"Does that mean what I think it means?" Lola asked her mother.

"I'm afraid it does," Mom said.

Lola looked at Grampa Ed. He didn't speak, but his face was unusually red.

"Are you OK, Grampa?" Lola asked.

Grampa Ed made a scraping noise in his throat that wasn't pleasant.

Grampa put his fork down on the table and asked Mom to read the letter again. When she got to the part about hairstyles causing distractions in some classes, Grampa broke in again: "What's wrong with a little distraction?" he asked. The question hung there in the air over the dinner table.

Lola was quiet for a long time. Everyone was quiet. Lola was thinking of *Charlotte's Web*, again. When Charlotte the spider was unhappy about a situation in the book, she used words to try to change it. Lola was unhappy with Mr. Murch's new pigtails rule. Could she, Lola, use words to change the situation at school?

Finally, Lola broke the silence: "I think Mr. Murch is wrong," she said. She paused. "Can I tell him that?"

She looked at her mother and she looked at her grandpa. She thought she saw a smile on her grandpa's face, but she wasn't sure.

"What do you want to tell him?" Mom asked.

"I want to tell him I think he's making a mistake. I think pigtails are fun, and what's wrong with school being fun? I want to ask him if the kids can vote. I bet the kids would vote for fun pigtails and ponytails.

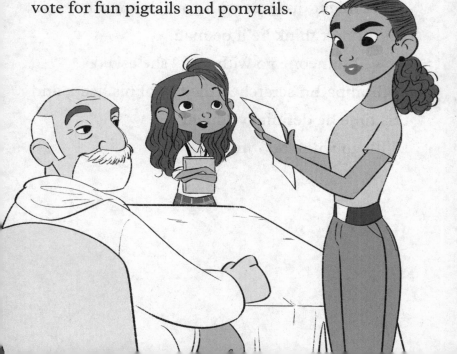

I bet even Mr. Murch would vote for fun pigtails and ponytails if he had long hair and he knew how awesome they were."

Mom asked: "Lola, are you going to say all that to Mr. Murch? Are you going to go into his office and ask him if you can vote?"

Lola rubbed her chin and thought about it. "Would I get in trouble?" she asked.

"No, if you're respectful and polite, Mr. Murch will listen," her mother said.

"Will Mr. Murch be mad?" she asked.

"He might disagree with you," her mother said, "but I don't think he'll be mad."

"Will someone go with me?" she asked.

Grampa Ed scratched the top of his head, and this time he definitely smiled.

"I'll go with you," he said.

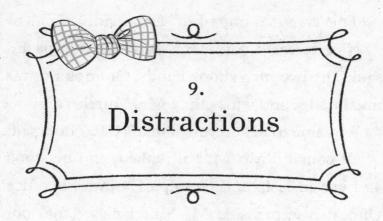

9.
Distractions

On the first day back to school after the winter break, Grampa Ed walked Lola to school early. They went straight to the principal's office.

"Lola Jones and Ed Jones would like to see Mr. Murch, please," Grampa Ed said to the secretary at the desk.

Just then Mr. Murch stepped out of his office and saw Lola standing with her grandfather. Mr. Murch was a small man with an egg-shaped face and a pointy chin. He wore a blue shirt and a green tie.

"Good morning, Lola," Mr. Murch said. He looked at Grampa.

"This is my Grampa Ed," Lola said.

"Nice to meet you, Mr. Murch," Grampa Ed said. The two men shook hands. Grampa Ed was much taller and wider than Mr. Murch.

"We came to talk to you, if that's OK," Lola said.

"Of course," Mr. Murch replied, and he stood and waved Lola and Grampa Ed into his office. Once they were inside, Mr. Murch closed the door.

Everyone sat down.

"What can I do for you?" Mr. Murch asked.

Grampa Ed looked at Lola. Lola took a deep breath and looked straight at Mr. Murch.

"Um, Mr. Murch," she said, "I was hoping you would change your mind and let us wear pigtails. I mean, not just ordinary pigtails, but even the crazy ones."

"I see," Mr. Murch said. "And why do you feel so strongly about it, Lola?"

"Well, because they're fun," Lola said. "And they make us feel special. And you said in your letter that the uniform is good because it saves money. And pigtails and ponytails are totally free—and they're good for preventing lice. And also because I think the kids should get to vote if the rules are going to change, and..."

Lola ran out of words. She could feel her heart beating in her chest. Talking to the principal was harder than she thought.

Grampa Ed placed his hand on Lola's shoulder, for encouragement, and that made her feel a little better.

Mr. Murch smiled, but it wasn't really a happy smile.

"Well, Lola," he said. "I appreciate your opinions. We think all our students are special no matter how they dress. But our main job is to teach our children, and we can't do that if there are too many distractions."

Grampa Ed started to make a scraping noise in his throat that wasn't pleasant, but Lola cut him off. She remembered what her mother said about being respectful and polite. She thought about the polite way Charlotte always spoke to Templeton the rat in *Charlotte's Web*, and she chose her next words carefully: "May I please ask you a question?" she asked.

"Of course," Mr. Murch said.

"What's wrong with a little distraction?"

"I'm not sure I understand," Mr. Murch said.

Grampa started to laugh, but he pretended to cough to cover it up.

"I mean, kids are always going to get distracted," Lola said. "We're distracted by passing notes to

each other, or a bird at the window, or smells from the cafeteria, or someone sneezing—or coughing," Lola said, glancing at Grampa. "And pigtails aren't *that* distracting. So why don't you let us vote on them?"

"I don't think a vote is appropriate in this case," Mr. Murch said. "I think we know how the students would vote. This is my decision."

"And is there any way we can change your mind?" Lola asked.

"I'm sorry, but no," Mr. Murch said. "Any other questions?"

"Not yet," Lola said, rubbing her chin, "but I'm sure I'll think of something."

"I'm afraid my decision stands." Mr. Murch put his hands on his desk.

Lola looked at her grandfather, hoping he would say something. He gave her a wink, but he didn't speak.

"C'mon, kid," Grampa Ed said finally, standing up. "Let's go. Good day, Mr. Murch."

When they were outside in the hall, Lola stopped walking and looked up at her grandfather.

"Why didn't you help me?" she asked. "Why didn't you say something?"

"You didn't need my help, honey," Grampa Ed said. "You were great. You were really brave and really smart. Made me proud."

"But I lost," she said.

Grampa's face loosened, and he bent over until his nose was almost touching Lola's.

"Trust me, kid, you didn't lose."

"Yes, I did. I lost."

"Well, you don't have to quit. If you want to keep pushing for pigtails, you keep pushing, and I'll help. It might be fun."

"How?" Lola asked.

Grampa smiled.

"Distractions," he said.

10.
Hatching a Plan

The next day at school, Lola wore her white shirt and blue skirt, as usual. But she had no pigtails, no ponytails, no jewelry, not even striped socks.

"My underwear is plain white, too," she whispered when she met Maya and Fayth in front of her apartment. "I'm trying to make myself almost invisible. I don't want Mr. Murch or anybody else to pay attention to me until I hatch my plan!"

"Oooh, you're hatching a plan?" Fayth said. "That sounds so exciting!"

"Can we help?" asked Maya.

"It is kind of exciting, but kind of scary too,"

Lola said. "And, yes, you can definitely help. I *need* you guys."

"Awesome!" said Fayth. "What's the plan?"

The girls whispered as they walked to school. When they reached the playground gate, Grampa Ed handed Lola a big, brown envelope.

"Good luck, kid," he said.

Lola nodded and gave her grandpa a hug. She turned to her friends.

"OK, guys," she said. "Let's split up these flyers. There's one for each kid in our class. Hand out

as many as you can before everyone goes in the building."

The girls said they understood, and they began running around the playground handing out the flyers until almost all were gone.

"We can do the rest at recess or after school," Lola said.

When the bell rang, all the children went inside. When Mrs. Gunderson took attendance, she almost marked Lola absent.

"I didn't notice you," the teacher said. "You look different today. Did you get a haircut?"

"No," Lola said. "But I don't have pigtails today. Maybe that's why you didn't notice me." She peeked at Fayth and Maya and smiled.

By the time recess came around, all the kids in third grade and lots of kids in other grades knew about Lola's flyers. She didn't have enough copies for kids in other grades. "But you don't really need the flyers," she said again and again to anyone who asked. "You know what to do tomorrow, right?"

Everyone knew what to do.

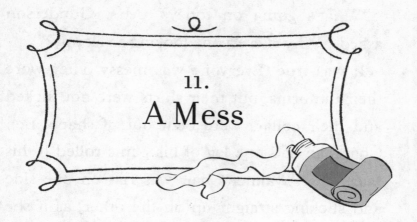

11.
A Mess

The following morning, the children entered the classroom and hung up their coats and put their lunches in the lunch bin. They sat down and slid their chairs in under their desks. Mrs. Gunderson looked up and made a funny face. There was something different about her classroom today. Everyone was quiet. That was unusual. But there was something else.

Mrs. Gunderson began to take the attendance, starting with Anthony Adducci and then moving on to Lisa Brown and on and on through the alphabet. When she got to Fayth Rogers, she stopped.

"What's going on today?" Mrs. Gunderson asked. "Why is everyone looking so sloppy?"

It was true. Everyone was messy. They wore their uniforms, but their shirts were not tucked and their collars were bent out of shape. Ben Chapman had one leg of his pants rolled to his knee. Terri Wallner's hair was flat on one side and sticking straight up on the other, as if she had just rolled out of bed. The buttons on Lola's shirt were in the wrong buttonholes and she had toothpaste on her chin. Maya was wearing mismatched shoes. Fayth had sidewalk chalk all over her pants. Peter Pincus's shirt was sticking out of the open fly of his pants (although, to be honest, that happened to Peter Pincus a lot).

No one answered when Mrs. Gunderson asked what was going on, but some of the children giggled and a few began talking. One person blurted out: "It's a day of distraction!" Lola hoped that Mrs. Gunderson didn't hear that.

"OK, let's settle down," Mrs. Gunderson said. "I don't know why you've all come to school

looking so messy, but we're going to get on with our work and I expect everyone to behave."

The class went quiet. Everyone loved and respected Mrs. Gunderson. They would never want to do anything to make her angry. The children behaved beautifully, even if they looked awful.

When the school day was over, Mrs. Gunderson asked Lola if she would stay behind for a minute to talk. The teacher waited until all the other children were gone.

"Is that toothpaste on your chin, Lola?" she asked.

"Yes."

"Did you have toothpaste for breakfast?"

"No," Lola said, "I just smeared some on there before I left for school."

"That's what I thought," Mrs. Gunderson said. "Would you like to tell me why you did that? And why everyone was so messy today?"

"Do I *have* to?" Lola asked.

"No, you don't," Mrs. Gunderson said. She smiled and looked at Lola. "But I think I have an idea of what's going on. Anyway, you have a nice evening. And, if you don't mind, would you give another letter to your grandfather for me, please?"

"Sure!" Lola said. "He really likes your letters."

"And I like his drawings."

"Why don't you guys just send text messages like everyone else?" Lola asked.

"Oh, but I think text messages are dreadful," Mrs. Gunderson said. "They're such *distractions*... don't you think?"

"Um," Lola said. "I...guess they are...um... *distractions*."

When Lola got home that afternoon, she stopped at Grampa Ed's studio first.

"How did the first day of your plan go?" Grampa Ed asked.

Lola smiled big. "It was awesome! We had so much fun. The teachers knew something was going on, but they didn't know what it was exactly. Wait until they see what we're going to do tomorrow."

"That's great," Grampa Ed said. "It's nice to see kids so excited about school."

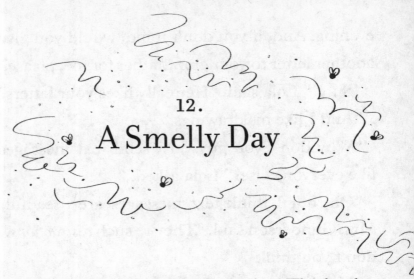

12.
A Smelly Day

These were the Days of Distraction. That's what Lola and Grampa Ed called their plan to change Mr. Murch's mind about pigtails and ponytails.

After Messy Day came Face Paint Day. Lola painted her entire face green. Fayth drew whiskers on her cheeks so she looked look like a cat. Maya painted on a clown mask. Some of the boys drew mustaches and beards, and some of them smudged black paint under their eyes so they looked like football players.

After that came Sunglasses Day. Then Fake Tattoo Day. On Fake Tattoo Day, Grampa Ed drew a pair of braided pigtails that almost covered

Lola's entire right arm. On her left arm he wrote in black ink: "IS THIS A DISTRACTION?"

The next day was Friday and it was the craziest day of them all: Really Bad Smell Day. Everyone arrived at school smelling as awful as they possibly could. The children ran around the classroom before the first bell sniffing their friends and trying to guess what was making each of them smell so awful.

"I brushed my teeth with garlic!" Ben Chapman shouted.

"I rubbed kitty litter on my shirt!" Tammy Logan said.

"I put tuna salad in my hair!" Garth Collins screamed.

"I used a whole bottle of my brother's cologne," Fayth said.

"I haven't had a bath in three weeks," Peter Pincus said.

When Lola pointed out to Peter that the Days of Distraction had only been going on for *one* week, Peter shrugged. "So?" he said. "What's your point?"

Everyone was laughing and shouting and sniffing and gagging when Mrs. Gunderson arrived. She walked a few steps into the classroom, stopped, and covered her nose and mouth with her hands.

"Oh, my!" she said, her voice low and muffled. "Oh, oh, my!"

She staggered to the window and opened it wide to let in some air. She looked at the children, who were dressed neatly in their uniforms, but who smelled like a garbage truck or a large family of frightened skunks.

"Listen carefully, class," she said. She coughed

twice and wiped her watering eyes. "Row one, please go to the restrooms and wash as well as you can to remove your foul odors. When row one returns, row two can go, followed by row three. Please do it quickly, class."

Lola was in row one, but before she could make it out the door, she heard Mrs. Gunderson's voice: "Lola, not you. Please come to my desk."

She wrote a note and handed it to Lola.

"Take this to Mr. Murch's office, please."

Lola swallowed hard and tried not to cry. She had never been sent to the principal's office before. Visiting Mr. Murch with Grampa Ed didn't count. This time felt like a punishment. Being the leader of the Days of Distraction made her feel important. It made her feel great. But now she wondered if all this was a bad idea. Would she get in

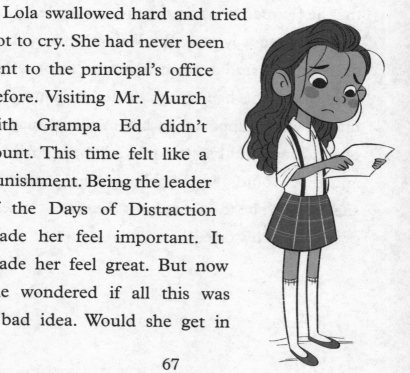

trouble? She felt scared and lonely, like Wilbur the pig when he first arrived in the Zuckermans' barn before he met Charlotte.

With her shoulders slumped and Mrs. Gunderson's note in her hand, Lola walked out of the classroom and down the hall to the principal's office. It was a long hallway, which gave Lola a chance to think. Last night, in the chapter of *Charlotte's Web* that Lola read before bedtime, Wilbur was so upset about something that he flopped down in the mud and cried. Lola felt the same way now. But Wilbur had the help of his friends and decided to give it his best shot. Lola knew she had to try to do the same. No matter what happened to her in the principal's office, Maya and Fayth would still be her friends, and they would always make her feel better. As she walked, she thought about *their* faces instead of Mr. Murch's face.

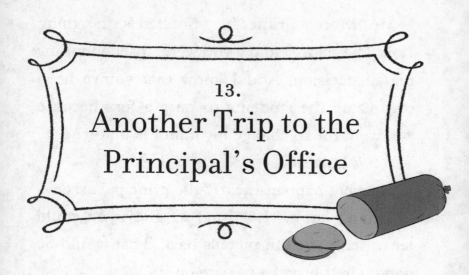

13.
Another Trip to the Principal's Office

"Well, Lola," Mr. Murch said. "It's been a very interesting week, hasn't it?"

Lola nodded, still trying not to cry.

"Would you like to tell me what's been going on?"

Lola shook her head, no. She knew if she spoke the tears would flow.

Mr. Murch waited for Lola. After a minute of silence, he made a funny face and asked: "Do you smell bologna?"

"Oh, that's me," Lola answered, patting her pockets.

Mr. Murch grimaced. "So here's the thing, Lola," he said. "I know you were upset about my pigtail decision. And I know that you've been organizing the students to raise a fuss because you want me to change my mind. Is that true?"

"Yes," Lola said.

"So what happens next?" the principal asked.

"I don't know," Lola said. "I guess you could let us have our fun pigtails back. That would be good. Or at least let us vote on it."

"And what if I don't?"

"Well..." Lola took a deep breath. "On Monday it's going to be Inside Out Clothes Day. On Tuesday it's going to be Whispering Day. On Wednesday I think we're going to do Really Bad Smell Day again because this one is really popular..."

"And what if I ask you to stop?"

"Well, I can't really stop, Mr. Murch, unless you give us a vote or give us the pigtails back. See, I've been telling my friends that we were doing this to show that kids have power. That we

can change things if we stick together. It's called persistence. I can't just stop. That would be giving up. Charlotte would never stop writing in her webs after she promised to save Wilbur's life!"

Mr. Murch lowered his pointy chin and looked at his hands.

"And what do you suppose would happen if we voted?" he asked.

"Well, Mr. Murch," Lola said. "I'm pretty sure

everyone would vote for fun pigtails. You can't really expect kids to vote for more rules, can you?"

"That's true," Mr. Murch said. "And that's why I made the decision on my own. I'm afraid the rule stays."

Lola rose from her chair and left the principal's office. She walked down the hall with her head down and her shoulders hanging low, and when she passed a garbage can, she removed the bologna slices from her pockets and threw them away.

14.
Pete and Repeat

The Days of Distraction continued. Inside Out Day was fun. Whispering Day was kind of boring. Really Bad Smell Day was really smelly but not as funny and not as smelly the second time.

"I think the Days of Distraction are going to be over soon," Lola told Grampa Ed one morning as she made his coffee and as Grampa Ed made a pair of plain pigtails for her hair.

"Does that mean you're giving up?"

"I don't *want* to," Lola said, "but I don't know what else to do."

"Well, what would that spider of yours do? The one from your book?"

"Charlotte? She'd use words," Lola said. "That's her secret power."

"Ever heard of a petition?" Grampa asked.

"I don't think Mom's going to let me have a pet," Lola said.

Grampa laughed.

"No," he said. "Not a pet...a *petition*. It's a humble request that you make in writing. You can use a petition to try to change a rule that's not fair."

"But I already tried to change Mr. Murch's mind! A letter's not going to help!"

"Well, maybe you can impress him by getting a lot of people to sign your petition."

"Petition. Petition. Petition." Lola rolled the word around in her mouth. "Hey, if you say it over and over it becomes repetition."

"I suppose it does."

"Petition...petition...petition...petition..."

"Can you stop saying that now, please?"

Lola kept saying *petition, petition, petition,* but she said it softly so her lips moved but Grampa Ed couldn't hear. Then she spoke up:

"Hey, Grampa. Pete and Repeat are in a boat. Pete falls out. Who's left in the boat?"

Grampa scratched his head. "Uh," he said. "Repeat."

"Pete and Repeat are in a boat. Pete falls out. Who's left in the boat?"

"Repeat."

"Pete and Repeat are in a boat. Pete falls out. Who's left on the boat?"

Grampa shook his head. He moaned as he rose from the edge of his bed.

"Go to school," he said.

"Who's left on the boat, Grampa?"

"Go to school!"

Lola giggled. "Who's left on the boat, Grampa?"

"You never give up, do you, kid?" Grampa chuckled. "The boat was attacked by a bunch of sharks and it sunk. Now go to school!"

15.
Petition and Repetition

Lola wrote a petition. It said:

Dear Mr. Murch,

    Our teachers say America is the land of freedom. We learn to celebrate that everyone is different and different is good. That's why rules about hairstyles don't make sense to us. We are signing this letter to say kids should have a choice about how they wear their hair. Teachers don't have to obey rules about how they wear their hair. Why should kids have to? We ask you to let kids vote on the rules. We think it's important to let kids and adults think for themselves and be creative. Do you agree? Please answer.

                                Your friends,

Lola, Maya, and Fayth spent all week asking students to sign their petition. There were 390 students in their school. By the end of the week, they had 400 signatures, because some teachers and janitors and cafeteria workers signed too.

One morning before the bell rang, Lola, Maya, and Fayth showed their petition to Mrs. Gunderson. They had fourteen pages of signatures attached. Some of the signatures were in crayon. Those were mostly the kindergarten kids.

"We want to take it to Mr. Murch," Maya told the teacher.

"But we're a little scared," Fayth added.

Mrs. Gunderson read the petition. She smiled.

"I'm proud of you," she said. "This is an excellent petition. Why don't you take it to the principal's office right now? I'm sure Mr. Murch won't mind."

"Do you think he'll change his mind about the pigtails and ponytails?" Lola asked.

"I don't know," Mrs. Gunderson said. She paused. "May I sign it?"

The girls said yes. Soon they were on their way to the principal's office, holding hands as they walked.

"You'll do all the talking, right?" Fayth squeezed Lola's hand.

"You can talk, too," Lola said.

"But he knows you already," Fayth said.

"And it was your idea, not ours," Maya added.

"OK," Lola said. "But you guys can definitely talk if you want to."

"How about if we nod our heads and say 'yeah' a lot?" Maya said.

"That's good," Lola said. "Act like you're really excited, OK?"

Fayth and Maya promised.

When they got to Mr. Murch's office, his door was closed but his secretary said the girls could knock and go in.

"Hello, girls," Mr. Murch said, looking surprised. "How can I help you today?"

Lola cleared her throat. "Mr. Murch, do you remember when I asked you if we could have a vote on the pigtails and ponytails?"

"Yes, of course I remember, Lola," Mr. Murch said. "And I'm sorry to say I haven't changed my mind. I'm not going to allow a vote."

"Well," Lola said, "since we couldn't vote, we decided to do a petition. It's a letter that makes a humble request. We got 401 signatures." She put the petition on Mr. Murch's desk. The principal picked it up and thumbed through the pages of signatures, then went back to the first page and read the letter Lola had written.

"This is very impressive," Mr. Murch said.

"Some of the teachers signed, too," Maya said.

"But mostly kids," Fayth said.

"Very impressive," Mr. Murch said.

"So what do you think, Mr. Murch?" Lola asked.

"Girls," the principal said, "I have to tell you that this is excellent work. This petition is well written, and you got the whole school to sign it. That wasn't easy. I think your bravery and your hard work should be rewarded. And ever since our last meeting, Lola, I've been thinking about what you said."

"You *have*?" Lola asked, sounding surprised.

"Yes, I have," Mr. Murch said. "And I have an idea. Tell me what you think."

The girls leaned forward to listen.

"What if we started something called Spirit Week?" Mr. Murch said. "During Spirit Week, students would pick different fun ways of dressing. They could have Pajama Day, Silly Hair Day, Sports Team Day, or whatever they want. The students can choose." He paused. "But not Smelly Day!"

The girls laughed.

"That sounds really fun," Lola said. "Could we have Spirit Week every month?"

"How about once a year?" Mr. Murch asked.

"How about six times a year?" Lola asked.

"How about four—one for each report-card period?" Mr. Murch said.

"Deal!" Lola said. She jumped out of her chair and shook the principal's hand. Then Maya and Fayth shook Mr. Murch's hand too.

"I'll send a letter home so the students know that their petition worked," Mr. Murch said.

Lola had a big smile on her face. She felt strong and proud.

Mr. Murch looked out the window and then back at Lola. He ran his hand over his bald head.

"I used to have beautiful curly hair, you know?" he said.

"Really?" the girls all said at once. Lola tried to picture it but couldn't.

"What color was it?" she asked.

"About the same as yours," he said. "One year I let it grow so long it touched my shoulders."

The girls started laughing hysterically. They couldn't help it. Fayth fell off her chair and hurt her elbow, but only a little.

"OK, calm down," Mr. Murch said. He stood up, helped Fayth up from the floor, and turned to the window. As he gazed outside he watched a small squirrel chase a bigger one. He turned back to the girls. "OK," he said, "so you can go crazy with pigtails during Spirit Week, but you'll keep them plain and simple the rest of the time, right?"

"Right!" Lola said. She couldn't wait to tell her mother and grandfather.

"Right!" Maya said.

"Right!" Fayth said. She added: "And, oh, by the way, Mr. Murch. I think you'd still look good with long hair. Maybe you should grow it out again."

"I'll give that some thought," Mr. Murch said with a smile. "Now, you girls should get back to class right away."

16.
Some Pigtails

When she got home from school, Lola shared her
news about the pigtails with Grampa Ed. She also
gave him another letter from Mrs. Gunderson.

Lola read it aloud:

Dear Ed,

When I was a little girl, my favorite book was <u>Charlotte's Web</u>. It's still my favorite, really. That's why I make sure my third graders read it in class. It contains so many life lessons for little people—and big people.

I've often wondered: Why did Fern ask her mother where her father was going with his ax? Surely it wasn't the first time she'd seen her father with an ax. He was a farmer. He probably killed pigs and chickens and geese all the time.

But Fern was curious. She wanted to know what was going on around her. She was not the kind of girl to eat her breakfast and stare at her cell phone while unfair things happened around her. She not only noticed, of course, she acted. She ran out to stop her father from killing the little pig. The first time I read the book, I thought it should have been called <u>Fern the Brave</u> instead of <u>Charlotte's Web</u>.

Anyway, it's been an eventful week at school. Lola did a lot of noticing and acting, as you probably know. And to think it's only January! Five more months of school to go!

Fondly,
Sandy Gunderson

Grampa Ed took a piece of paper from his desk drawer and started sketching.

He drew a spider web. Then he drew a spider at the bottom of the web. Then he drew pigtails on the spider.

"Here," Grampa said. "Write something on the web for me."

"What should I write?" Lola asked.

"Whatever you want," Grampa said.

Lola wrote in all capital letters and tried to make it look like the words were attached to the web. It said: "S-O-M-E P-I-G-T-A-I-L-S."

After dinner that night, Lola's mother suggested a trip around the corner for ice cream.

"We should celebrate Lola's bravery," Mom said, "and how she stood up for her beliefs and organized the petition. I'm proud of you, honey."

"We should celebrate your new job, too, Lillian," Grampa Ed said to Lola's mother. "I'm proud of both of you."

"I'm proud of you, Mom," Lola said. "And you, too, Grampa. We should celebrate your new talent as a hairdresser!"

Grampa Ed gave her a crooked smile.

"We can also celebrate this," Lola said, holding up her book. "I finished *Charlotte's Web*!"

The days grew longer. The dirty snow that lined the sidewalks began to melt and puddle and slide down the sewer grates. The trees grew buds. Tiny blades of grass sprouted from patches of dirt. New life spread across the city. Children put their heavy coats in their closets and took their baseball gloves, scooters, and bicycles out of their basements.

One day during spring break, Grampa Ed invited Mrs. Gunderson to go to a diner for lunch.

On the last day of vacation, Lola got a haircut. The hairdresser wove her hair into two elaborate French braids.

"Do you like them?" she asked Grampa Ed.

"Very impressive," he said.

"I can teach you how to make them if you want," Lola said. "Wouldn't that be fun?"

"Not really," he said.

Even so, every morning that spring, Grampa Ed helped Lola with her hair. Sometimes he made pigtails, sometimes he made ponytails, and sometimes he made classic French braids—with minty gum wrappers threaded in.

In the afternoons, Lola did her homework while sitting next to Grampa Ed at his drawing table. Sometimes she picked up pencils and made her own sketches. Sometimes she wrote little stories to go along with her pictures.

"Hey, Grampa," Lola said one day. "Did I tell you I started reading a new book?"

"No," Grampa said. "What's it called?"

"*Anne of Green Gables*," Lola said. "Mrs. Gunderson recommended it. It's about an orphan girl with red hair who goes to live with two adults who don't have any children. They really want a boy, but they get a girl by mistake and they're not sure they want to keep her. Oh, and she talks too much and uses big, fancy words."

"You're not going to want red hair, are you?"

"Maybe." Lola giggled.

"You're not going to start using a bunch of big, fancy words that I can't understand, are you?"

"Hmmm," Lola said. "What's a big, fancy word for *maybe*?"

She paused and rubbed her chin.

"I've only read two chapters so far," she said. "But I wonder how Anne learned all those words."

"Maybe she had a thesaurus."

"No, Grampa, it's an old book, but it's not that old. There are definitely no dinosaurs in Green Gables!"

Grampa laughed.

"A thesaurus is not a dinosaur," he said. "It's a book of synonyms. It helps you find just the right word for whatever you want to say."

Lola's eyes went wide.

"Oh, that's a great idea! I'm going to the library tomorrow and I'm going to get a thesaurus! A big one! A brontosaurus-sized one!"

She grabbed a sheet of paper and began writing words to look up in the thesaurus. She wrote: *synonym*, *maybe*, *smelly*, *radiant*, *funny*, and *gables*.

"Wow, this is not going to be easy," Lola said. "But…" She twirled her pencil. "But it *is* going to be fun!"

Jonathan Eig is as bald as a lightbulb, but he's had a lot of practice making pigtails for his daughters. He likes pigtails so much he decided to write a book about them. Jonathan is a *New York Times* bestselling author and award-winning journalist whose most recent book was a biography of Muhammad Ali. He's currently working on a biography of Martin Luther King, Jr. and writing more books about Lola Jones. He lives in Chicago with his wife, three children, and a hamster named Cheerio. *Some Pigtails* is his first book for children.

Alicia Teba Godoy is from Barcelona where she studied cinema and illustration and was very influenced by storytelling and fairy tales. She is passionate about drawing, animals, and cinema. She has illustrated books, stationery, comics, children's magazines, and even concept arts, but loves illustrating children's literature most of all. Like Lola Jones, Alicia is determined and, also like Lola, who stole her heart, Alicia is always creating and coming up with new ideas. Visit @garbancita_alicia on Instagram to learn more.